THREE TALL TALES

by the same author

Miserable Love Poetry and Other Poems (2022)

The Deathbed Poet and Other Poems (2023)

Three Tall Tales

**ANTHONY
WHITE**

Mislove Publishing

CONTENTS

FOREWORD

"Truth is stranger than fiction, but it is because Fiction is obliged to stick to possibilities; Truth isn't." (Mark Twain, Following the Equator: A Journey Around the World)

'A tall tale is a story that is very difficult to believe: a greatly exaggerated story' (Webster's Dictionary). My premise is that all tales are tall tales. The moment a writer puts pen to paper, fingers to keyboard, the very acts of selection, compression, understatement become in themselves a kind of exaggeration- these events, these conversations, are the important ones, the writer seems to say; all the other things that happened to these people are not. And how often do we, reading or hearing stories, say "I can't/won't/don't believe it"? (-Did you know that X has died? -I don't believe it. I saw him only last week.)

In these days, we find stories difficult to believe both because we sense that they are exaggerated, and that we know things have been left out. We are not being told the whole story.

In this volume, The Artists Who Burned a Million Quid is an 'I can't believe it' story. It is, however, true. In The Thing With Harry, the narrator can hardly believe that a few banal events from his youth continue to matter; more, have defined the course of his life. In Two Versions, the narrator finds the story too much for him. He feels he should do something, but can't, for the life of him, think what.

Tall tales tell truths? Good God, one hopes they do, but what truth is and if it matters is another story.

THE ARTISTS WHO BURNED A MILLION QUID

In the early hours of the morning
Of August 23rd, 1994,
Bill Drummond and Jimmy Cauty, burning
A million quid of fifty-pound notes- more
Money than most artists ever see.
They had flirted with the idea before,
That money has become the root of art-
How beautiful is money? was the core.
Why paint Sunflowers, Nativities, nude sweethearts?
No artist needs to hear the Muses' call
To understand that the activity
Is just like nailing money to a wall.
Therefore, what kind of art could be purer
Than burning a million quid on the Isle of Jura?

More than news of murders and poverty,
Corruption in the corridors of power,
New crime waves, stabbings and armed robbery,

The photograph of three men around a fire
Drinking whisky from the bottle, poking
Bundles of fifty-pound notes with a stick
To catch a flame, and, it appears, not joking-
No, they look more as though they're feeling sick;
More than news of footballers and of sex,
Columnists explaining what these events mean,
The extinction of species, plane crash wrecks,
The disgrace of someone who once met the Queen,
More than all the bad news in the world
This was the baddest news that could be heard.

There should, I think, have been an audience,
And I don't mean the kind of audience
Made up of those who already have the key
Or have at least sometime have touched the key,
People who are always in the audience,
Who use words such as 'horizontality'.
No, I mean an audience of families;
Fathers carrying children on their backs
Saying You'll Never See The Like Of This Again;
Mothers, grandparents, widows, families
Who've done nothing like this since who-knows-when?
There's nothing like a fire in the outback
In the dark to attract an audience,
Who talk of life, of art and of mortality.

The population of Jura, give or take,
Is two hundred, few of them millionaires.
A million quid (the difference that could make,

Five thousand each!) would relieve a few cares,
But would that be creative, thought-provoking,
Controversial, challenging, satirical?
Five thousand quid is neither here nor there
But burning a million quid can really change things.
It can change your life, like a miracle,
It can ruin it, have you waking in the glare
Of day thinking What Have I Done?
If love of money's the root of all sin
What of this hatred of money they slung
In the fire with their yan and their yin?

How much they preferred their lost memories
Of sunflowers, nativities, naked flesh,
With their attendant ghosts of shame and regret,
To this piece of work that cannot be lost
(There are photographs, a journalist's account).
They lose their hands in the ashes of the fire.
Ars longa vita brevis- but the amount?
Is art too long, life too short for
All the forgetting and spending that must be done?
Van Gogh and Rembrandt died broke, their money gone
And now their works sell for two hundred million.
Is life too short to spend two hundred million?
Where would you find the time for the lost memories
With their attendant ghosts of regret and shame?

On August 23rd 1994
In the early hours of the morning
In an abandoned boathouse on Jura

Drummond and Cauty sat there burning
A million in fifty-pound notes in the fire
On the second day they created light
On the third divided the waters from the sky
On the fourth they created day and night
And then the sun and moon to light the earth
The plants and living creatures and then Man
And then created money and its worth
And said to man Do with it what you can
You only live one life there's nothing surer
So come and join in the fun on the Isle of Jura

If you don't know this story and would like to find out more, type K Foundation Burn a Million Quid into your browser and you will find all sorts of stuff. Too much to list here, except to say that 'nailing money to a wall' was one of their previous artworks.

THE THING WITH HARRY

We've only one virginity to lose,
And where we lose it there our hearts will be
Rudyard Kipling, The Virginity

There were ever so many girls called Harry at that time. I tell you this in case you think I'm making it up, trying to make her sound unusual, like a person you might want to read about. But it's true- her name was Harry and there were lots of them then. The name shot up the charts the way the original did- Harry Jones, the girl from, unprecedentedly, Totnes, who captured the nation's heart with her string of number ones (eight, was it?), her five (four? six?) husbands, her year in detox, her comeback, critically acclaimed album that didn't sell, cancer. You remember. Harriet, of course, but Harry.

The one I knew was a Harriet-but-Harry. She tried breaking free once, told everyone to call her Hal, but it never took. She was nineteen, a year older than I was at the time- and before and since of course, unless she has died, which she might have, nobody lives forever- and a bold, upright, slim, long-haired (black her hair, I want to say, but I don't suppose it was truly black, probably deep brown, that's the more usual thing isn't it? and what now? grey? white? ah! spare me), smiling, clever, not-easily-taken-in, promiscuous nineteen-year-old woman who taught me a thing or two, though I no longer remember if it was only the one thing, or if I got the two; and, besides, I have long, much longer, forgotten what either of them were. But she was a grand girl, yes, but me no buts, she was, never mind all I said before about her up-rightness and promiscuity, she was, tout en tout, a grand girl. Woman.

It was her bold confidence that appealed to me most no it wasn't it was her willingness to take me to her room pour toute la nuit but other than that it was her bold confidence; less so her slyness, which manifested itself at the last, at the time we were throwing pots and pans at each other; no, I'm missing a small detail here, it was she throwing the pans, I was ducking. Yes, she was a proper fury when it counted, swearing and shouting and accusing, like a harridan or harpy or fishwife even. Most of it standard stuff, I realised after a few- several- similar experiences over the years; standard and unimaginative- the guerre à mort after the petites morts. Had I had a backlog of such experiences at the time, rather than being a virgin in these matters, I would have egged her on. Come on, you can do better than that, that sort of thing. Well, she could actually, as it turned out, because in the middle, or perhaps at the climax of her harangue, she yelled, screeched I think, or shrieked, AND I saw what you wrote in your diary about Lily you dirty bastard you never loved me at all. Well of course I didn't love her. I thought I did, and said I did, but why ever would she believe such nonsense? She was a year older than I, for goodness' sake. Yes, it must have been at the climax because I remember now that, having shrieked herself out and got the thing about Lily out of her system, she burst into tears and threw herself into my arms. And then the rest.

The point is or was that she had read my diary, or journal as I called it, in which I had confessed- no, stop, wait a minute, I do make myself laugh sometimes, what am I saying 'confessed'? It wasn't a confession, it was a lubricious, late-night, alcohol-fired sexual fantasy. With a basis of reality. My feelings for Harry's best friend and roommate Lily, an unintellectual- studying English Literature I seem to recall, unless I am wrong- woman adorned, from head to toe, with striking features in a way Harry, who, don't misunderstand me, was pretty enough, and, you know, fit, was not. And the point was, yes, I've got there at last, you only have to be patient, that Harry had come across this in my journal and said nothing about it at the time but had stored it up and hurled it at me along with the cups and saucers and the tonguelashings at a moment when it was impossible, both physically and mentally, for me to throw back at her What the fuck were you doing reading my journal, you bitch? You had to admire her.

Can they be any use, these memories? They come at any time, sometimes willed, sometimes unwilled, unwanted, cursed even- Why plague me still after all this time? But, yes, sometimes willed, even tender enough to make me wish or wonder if, were we to meet by chance- chance it would have to be ; design out of the question- there would still be, finally be, something to be consummated. Love, I mean. Yes, that must be the question that is out of the question; the thing of great moment that lasts but a moment. Was it, and therefore is it, is it still, or yet, the thing called Love? I ask because you'd think I'd know wouldn't you by now but I don't and nor did you. For it seems to me no that when it comes to Love there are two kinds of people in the world, the one kind those who love and the love grows, the other those who have only a quota of love and once they have used it up it's gone and they have only the rest of their lives to use up somehow. Does that answer your question, if you had one? Yes the memories can come at any time and never more so than when I hear, some-times by chance, sometimes by choice, one of those great songs of Harry Jones- Où sont les neiges d'antan, perhaps. Or the one called- you must know it - You Read Me Like A Book. I can't bear it.

Funny, you would think, to keep finding yourself the centre of your own attention after all this time; centre of the universe. Surely by now I should have realised my folly and given everything away to my daughters, devoted myself to others; think of all those millions worse off than I. Instead, I find myself thinking, absurdly, of Lily. Absurd because I can't remember at all what she looked like, how she spoke and what she talked about; am uncertain if her name was, is, actually Lily; more uncertain, as if I had cared, that she was an Eng Lit student, rather than Geography or P.E. For all I know she's a cabinet minister or a bishop, though more likely, very much more likely, a teacher. A teacher and a mother. In fact,

I'd bet a million pounds she became a teacher, not that I have a million pounds floating about waiting for me to gamble it, but you know what I mean. No, she, Lily- Lulu? Linda?- was more of a shade, always there, always trustworthy, but unknown, unremembered or at best half- or a bit- remembered, but definitely not as much as half, more like a tenth or even twentieth, if that. Only her name, or something approximate, and the desire. Lily, I think. Almost sure.

I could have wept, as people say. They do say it: consider: We were two-nil up with three minutes to play and we lost- I could have wept. The man in the coonskin cap wants eleven dollar bills and I've only got ten; I could have wept. All the time you hear this and, even when, in extremis, I use the phrase myself, it cuts no ice with me, it butters no parsnips. For, Good Lord, to fall short like that, to fail to go through with weeping when you could have wept! What a falling short was there, and having once fallen, I fear, one keeps falling. I wouldn't weep then, and cannot now. I shall take these secrets to the grave, which is lunacy- what does my grave want with them? In my defence- and I am bereft of other defenders, for the dozens, scores of people who willingly, unthinkingly, naturally would wish to speak in my defence, can only get the wrong end of the stick, for what do they know of the secrets I am reserving for my grave? What would make them think that I need defending?- and I think this, if not a clincher, a persuasive point; in my defence I would say, am saying, No-one ever invited me to weep. No-one, not a one, and absolutely not one at the time of which I have been writing. The idea of it would never have occurred to Harry, even, pragmatic soul that she was, intimate though we were- as if intimacy counts for anything in matters such as these- and as for Lily (Lola? Laura?), well, Lily probably didn't even know my name, no, now I'm exaggerating, she must have known it for a little while, but for no or not much longer than that. She wouldn't have known, for example, even had she guessed, which she might have done, even if only from general principles, how much I would have liked to get her by herself and invite her out of her clothes. But weep? No; whatever would have given her that idea?

I could have wept but didn't ergo I couldn't. I could have wept for joy, could have wanted, that is, to be able honestly to say such a thing, no, exactly that thing. These days it is required to submit one's details to the Disclosure and Barring Service when applying for certain types of employment, defi- nitely those kinds where children are involved- scoutmaster, dinner-lady and so on, but also I imagine some concerned with adults. I would say vulnerable adults, but that would mean everyone. Fortunately, we didn't have this in my day, other- wise who knows what might have become of me. Not that there was anything serious to disclose in my case, but there is a phrase they use- Other relevant information disclosed at the Chief Police Officer(s) discretion, and what discretion he, she or they have to exercise, I do not know. Heaven only knows. And just think- what if Lily were the Chief Police Officer? Rationally, I don't think there was, among my many character flaws and peccadilloes and venial sins, anything that would give any would-be employer doubts or second thoughts, let alone an absolute forbiddance or prohibition.

No, nobody ever thought it out of the question to employ me, or admit me to their circle, or thought it in question that I am beyond the pale or unemployable or should be in jail. No, nothing like that, but even so, Disclosure- no! Enhanced Disclosure!- who could survive such a thing? I mean what if Harry had come forward and told them, the Chief Police Officer(s), why she had found it necessary, or impossible not to throw pots and pans at me? And what if Lily had told them my true motive? They wouldn't have had to call in Maigret or Moriarty to work out how to deal with me. And I could have said nothing in my defence. Not a word.

Before all this there was childhood, and it is hard to connect the I I have been telling you about with the wee little lad I was just before. Well, childhood, it is either nothing or something to do with this. I ran the gamut, as all children do, and I see no point in going into detail. My parents were decent, but for the beatings; the food was good, except when I hated it; friendships were instructive, as were the betrayals; schools were places where you learned to smoke without getting caught. A note on betrayal, for that was a childhood lesson of utmost importance, and the elements of it didn't have to be learned, they simply became stuck, irremovably- the money, the kiss, the guilt, the return of the money, the suicide. Difficult for all of us to enact all of these elements, but we did our best, and, this being a lesson for life, still, I am certain, do.

I suppose I have a first memory. It is of course of my mother rocking me to sleep with that beautiful lullaby Help

Me Little Bitty Baby Help. I must have been about thirteen or fourteen, and it's a beautiful start in life to have a memory like that of mother and child. All shall be well you'd think after a start like that. I had had good teachers too, in the Primary School, St. Immaculata of the Inquisition R.C. (I believe they have changed the name now- it is something inspiringly innocuous such as Good Beginnings). I was considered promising, although promising-but-backward, with my insatiable need to be suckled. Yes, I would forsake all of the midday pleasures of marbles, skipping, running around aimlessly, to have a suck at the breast. And I suppose this must have been thought unusual, because they were always at the house- Miss St.Vincent, Miss di Angelo, Miss Pennant; even Miss O'Fogarthy, who was well beyond suckling age, came to tell Mummy and Daddy what a promising boy I was, she had never known, not in seventy years of teaching, a child of such promise, all I needed was to be steered in the right direction and the world was my oyster- Oxford, Cambridge, the Civil Service, or, and her old dry eyes lit up, a teacher! Perhaps I would get to be a headmaster! The headmaster of this very school! She must have thought this, her little joke, a great joke, and she laughed, insomuch as she was able to raise a laugh, which was not much. Anyway, the whole caboodle lay there before me, if only they, Mummy and Daddy, would nurture me, encourage me, hit me with a stick if I weakened. Yes, they were the boys. They could do it. I think that's what she said.

Ah! Childhood, what a Disneyland of trouble, from the bedwetting to the petty theft, with all the macabre in-between, and the beneficent God Mickey looking down at everything I did, and smiling and waving and while not exactly forgiving- he has not such powers- tolerant, patient, approving even. For most of that everlasting period, between the arrival of self-consciousness and the beginnings of egotism, introspection, self-absorption, all the necessaries of childhood, it never entered my head to think I must remember this, I must write it all down. Remember it? Write it down? Why would you?

I notice that I have mentioned beatings, and since I have, I cannot glide past or over the mention. Anyone who has stayed with me this long will undoubtedly be brought up short and want to know more, naturally such a person will want to know if this shaped my life, ruined my life, formed my character, scarred me for life. Such a person will want to know, possibly sympathetically or empathetically or academically, but I think even more possibly with pulse beginning to race, pupils enlarged, saliva appearing at the lips, tumescence occurring, if I too became a beater, a sadist or masochist or a specialist in both. Though not a savage beater, my father was driven not to excess, but still beyond his normal measure, which was a single, hard smack on the bottom with his carpet slipper, bedroom slipper, whichever it was, by my refusal, even while wailing and writhing with pain, tears flooding my face, choking, to admit what I had done and apologise. This was what made him keep at it, but, poor man, he never really had the stomach for it. He had more important things to do and couldn't be wasting his time and his energy, not to mention his slippers, trying to bring me into line. What's more, there was my mother to consider. Not that she disapproved,

I don't think that, she was the first to say Wait til your father gets home when one or the other of us had stretched her to the end of her tether, but it upset her to have to watch or listen to these performances, these dramas, and I think that my father thought that when he had arrived at the point where his face was red and his eyes were blazing and his teeth were bared, that this was not how he wanted her to see him. An ugly, comical drama it was, and I remain puzzled where it leaves me vis-a-vis the nature/nurture debate. A matter yet unresolved.

That, then, was childhood, and it brought me to the gates of life proper, like a green racehorse, fizzing with young energy and enthusiasm while at the same time having no notion how to fit my still unfurnished body into the starting stalls; all the same ripe as a pippin and ready for the first great defining love of my life, Whatshername. No, that's just making a silly joke; I know well enough what her name was and probably still is, but sometimes it slips my mind until it slips back in again. I say 'slips' because that is how it is, there is nothing I can do to force it. Anyway, Harry, diminutive of Harriett, putatively named after Harry (Harriett) Jones of Totnes, The Totnes Troubadour. Aka Hal.

The first time I felt the lash of Harry's tongue was when I said what a horrible car your mother drives. I should put that another way- "What a horrible car your mother drives". I never met her mother. Harry didn't want me to meet her, and that suited me fine. I had a mother of my own, and that was one too many. We were of that generation, you see, dumping the past, as quickly as it became the past, and that included mothers, into the dustbin of history, unless you needed to tap them for money or a new winter coat. The times were a-changing and the mothers must get off the road or at least into the slow lane while we sped by. So I couldn't have expected what happened when I said "What a horrible car your mother drives"- and it was horrible, a great long white car with rounded edges, not a hint of the rectilinear, and I think possibly with white wheels too; it was horrible, but more, it was an embarrassing car, one you wouldn't be seen dead in; of course not that, it was the direct opposite of the colour of car you would be happy to be dead in; whether you were driving to the cheap stand at the football ground, the jellied eel stall at Jaywick Sands, or, at the other end of the whatsit, to dine at The Savoy, or to a Royal garden party. I don't want to dwell on the subject, but it was a horrible car, it was a horrible car; there was no right place for it. So I was shocked, it made me laugh, when I saw this abominable thing pull up outside, and then saw Harry scampering towards it and greeting its driver with a kiss. I mean, she didn't even look ashamed or pull her scarf over her face. The lash of her tongue.

I should not, of course, have said it. Prior to the dwindling of youthful spirits, one didn't have the kind of ballpark psychology at readiness that would have told me that she, Harry, also thought it a horrible car, and that it was FOR THAT VERY REASON that she was so angry with me. Baffling, isn't it, now as then? The thought that I had spotted her mother's vulgarity, that I might start thinking O, that's where she comes from, she's the fruit of those loins, she's of that ilk, is she? was anathema to her. God knows what she raved; I was too terrified to take it in, but I remember a few How Dare Yous and one You Don't Know Me At All, the latter the thing that stuck in my mind and that I have no trouble recalling all these decades later. You don't know me. You've never taken the trouble to know me. You just want.

I hadn't expected this. Rows were something the dustbin generation had. We, the new generation, reserved our anger for more important matters than where did you put that and why aren't you ready yet and if I've told you once I've told you a thousand times; things like marching against the Vietnam war, apartheid, higher grants for students, though of course for higher grants not against them. So for her to tear a strip off me for taking the piss out of her mother's car was a lesson that made me doubt I'd ever learned anything, made me think I had better go back to the beginning, like in snakes and ladders. And then, and then, and I still find it impossible to understand this, even to believe it could have happened, before I had said anything in reply, before I had even muttered the word sorry, she burst into tears, threw her arms around me, kissed me, and sobbed on my shoulder for- well, for ever so long. Perhaps that was the moment the door opened, or possibly closed, and I had a glimpse, even a vision of what life, my life, was and would be like, what it amounted to. I remember guiding her trembling body to the bed, where we cemented our relationship. Me on top.

That was a lesson learned, or would have been had I understood what the lesson was, and what there was to learn from it. It's a mistake to think that you go up to university to learn from books and to get a good degree; you have also, more importantly, to learn from life. Not that I majored in any of the three- books, degree, life. It was my first big failure, letting myself down, letting everybody else down. I wasn't even sporty. I can't complain when I judge myself harshly about this, even though poor judgment has pockmarked every aspect of my life, so that I would find it impossible to look at a mirror and exhort myself Come on now! You're better than you think! or some such self-improving mantra. No, I've no right to complain, and no idea what the point of doing so might be. I can't have her back.

I had a friend called Stan, who had a moustache and who was from a lower class than I, so not a real friend. I was only humoring him, or he me. But he had money and used to stand me drinks, which was useful. I bring this back to mind because he is from the same epoch, the same stratum. I have heard nothing from him since then, and he is no more than a fossil in the cabinet of curiosities I call my memory, an exhibit that has simply gathered dust for decades. Perhaps his life has been a pleasant, fulfilling one, with good jobs and money, wives, children and so forth, whatever else he has wanted. Perhaps not. Perhaps he took to crystal meth and ended up in prison or rehab, although he didn't seem the type. But then who is? A type, I mean. After all, he had a moustache, and I don't remember there being other unbearded mustachios in my year. What type was he though? Can I remember? No, I can't. He was an average student, but did his work, knew how to enjoy himself, had an eye for the women, but all in all fairly average. What was it that drew us together for a time? I can't remember that either, but I suspect it was that he was an adult, and I still a child. An elder brother sort of a friendship then. Perhaps. Perhaps not. But he definitely had a black moustache, whereas I hardly needed to shave. O yes, and he had a car. I think I thought that terribly impressive. Could it have been that I was hitchhiking and he stopped for me? Could have. And might he have said If you're in no hurry, I thought we'd stop at this pub I know; I could do with a pint of beer and a sandwich; and then he did stop and he paid for everything? He might have. What a decent fellow he must have been, and why he put up with me I can't imagine, as he just taught me to be a scrounger, and to scrounge off him. It's not as though he was short of friends, he was popular enough, so there must have been something. Perhaps he liked me.

We were, though, accomplices, and perhaps he didn't have another. Our most famous and nerve-racking exploit was to steal the fire-extinguisher from the Great Hall. His pal at the bowling alley gave him twenty quid for it, which was not to be sneezed at in those days. I must have spent my share on booze, I can't think what else I would have done with it. I would hardly have bought something for my mother. Don't make me laugh.

I cannot for the life of me think why I've dragged poor Stan into this. It's not as if I ever or only occasionally remember him; he wasn't important in my life, but then given that life is not important, how could he have been? No, it's just that I'm remembering, and things pop up, all sorts of attendant waifs and strays rear their ugly heads. But for Stan to claim that he played an important part in my salad or hey days- during my seminal years, I mean- is monstrous. It's a joke. He must have had a disappointing subsequent fifty years to be battening on to my coat tails in this way, as though I were the most interesting thing that ever happened to him in his entire life. Come on now.

So Stan is no more than a cypher, although that opens up a can of worms, does it not? a cypher being both an unimportant thing or person and the key to the whole thing, the code, the whole caboodle, of salad, hey- and seminal days. I should ponder this, but all I can recollect are his moustache, car, money, and the cheerful scapegraceness that loosened his limbs. To what does that amount? I ask you.

You would think o here I go again you think why the hell and what for should I think about you think thought would think. Jesus. Okay, calm down. You would think I am trying to get at the truth and that I'm nowhere near it. Yes, that's it, only more- am I trying to get at the truth? Why should I?- it's bound to be horrible, so why in goodness name for heaven's sake go near it? Boring too, I bet ya. And I don't, I can be sure of this now at the age I am, I don't have the courage. But then who does? No-one I've ever known. You see I'm getting angry now and that's leading me astray. Anger, truth, courage, ye Gods, what am I thinking? Let's forget all that and get back to the matter in hand. What's the matter?

The matter is having some life left over. A day, a year, a

decade, twenty years, how can I know? Be a better person I tell myself, be kind, consider others not just yourself. Sounds simple but what if you can't stand other people? There's a thing, and if I am ever tempted to think that- no, experience that- what then am I supposed to think of myself? That some-thing is terribly wrong surely? And so I go back, to when I was innocent- no, no, I was never innocent; even before the age of seven I was bad, mischievous at best, naughty, venial sins I suppose- I never killed anybody, to give an idea what I mean- but ten years on, eleven, twelve let's say, to say that I was innocent then is ridiculous, and yet, and yet, that's how I see myself. Then.

I hadn't wanted to get on to death so quickly. It's a cheer-less topic, whatever your view of it, but then so is life if you look at it that way, most of us getting eighty years plus of it these days and able to remember what? A few hours of inci-dents, your wedding day for example, though why you have failed to blot that out is beyond any guess of mine; beyond reason. Not but what I don't dislike a good wedding, although not nearly as much as a good funeral. They are occasions when you can get good blind drunk and not mind at all, or not much, getting stuck in a corner with the cousin you've managed to avoid for twenty years, for as long as you've known him in fact, I put twenty years just as a for example. Yes, you can get blind drunk and be forgiven no matter how badly you behaved, as long as you didn't have your hand up the bridesmaid's skirt or up her anywhere else for that matter, because everyone, even the cousins, will allow that you must have deliriously happy (weddings) or very sad (funerals) and so you have a ready-made excuse, which is a great blessing for a drunkard, as it takes an unclouded mind as well as effort to think up plausible excuses, even specious ones. If they knew, or God-forbid saw, that that's what you are like all the other days of your life, with no ready-mades to excuse you- or bridesmaids, come to that- it would be another matter, but that's another matter entirely. God, I'm repeating myself, that's bad. I was talking about what one remembers but of course getting blind drunk at a wedding or funeral or any other day rules out the possibility of remembering, doesn't it? so I've somewhat destroyed my own argument, not that I had one, not that I was arguing. No-one to argue with.

Did I get on to death so quickly? Or at all? I can't re-member having brought it up, now I think of it. Am I dying, father? We're all dying, son. The old comedy routine- who was that lady I saw you with last night? That was no lady, I was alone. That was no lady, that was the priest with the extreme unction. Unction? Bunkum. Thank you thank you you're much too kind. No, seriously, I remember my brother said I'm sorry to hear your mother-in-law died; what was the complaint? And I said We haven't any. Death, though, is not funny, is it? When I moved house I asked the estate agent What's the death rate around here? He said One per person. No, you've got to laugh, haven't you? Or you wouldn't.

But before death, which you'd have to think is all we have, is what persists and has you asking what did I have what did I do who was I what was it all about although when it comes to the point unction, the thing itself- you've probably stopped worrying your little head about all that palaver. Only when the relatives come and hold your hand and mutter soft words such as There there and ask the doctor in muffled tones How long O Lord How long does it prod once again the scab the scar the open wound of a life you only half-remember, not even half, only bits, fragments, an album of sepia photographs that look attractive at half-glance, first glance, better anyway than the pictures in your head, until you notice at full glance, second glance and so on, the teeth, the eyes, the strange postures, the looks of distrust apparent behind the smiles, the seas, the bright blue skies, the white buildings on those Mediterranean coasts. Sepia. What does it mean? Old brown photographs of the past. Another's past. Your grandparents, great-grandparents, people who died in The War. At the going down of the sun we will. Remember?

Sometimes so often I take shelter under the bedclothes, pillows on top of my head and everything, only to find to my horror or perhaps dismay that I don't sleep, I wake, what's more I still see, even inside all the wrappings. I still feel pain. It is then that I give up hope, although never quite all, there always seems to remain a little, for what it's worth. At least you hope there is a little bit of hope, that the sun will be shining when you wake, not that you've slept, but that when you drag the pillows reluctantly off your head the sun will shine on your face and feed you the illusion that it's worth springing out of bed, kidding yourself for the umpteenth time that life is worth living, doing your twenty press-ups, eating a breakfast and so on until about halfway through the morning you begin to deteriorate and it all begins again, the thought that you'd better be dead and all that goes along with that. Yes, it can change in a moment, or if not that, in a morning- love of life to wish of death. I can't think what it is I do to effect that turnaround, it comes upon me regardless. I have only to empty the last mouthful- no, not mouthful, that would be a mad way to drink it; no, last gulp, last inch, that will do- of coffee and I'm there, enervated or innervated whichever it is, but lost, definitely, to any notion of Life! Life as a good thing, a blessing, a word or an idea to start the adrenaline flowing and have you thinking I could do anything today, I'm a free agent, I could walk to Wales write a chapter buy a luxury lunch drink champagne pick up a woman no stop now you're being ridiculous, you don't need to be saying that. You're rethinking of Harry again. Don't.

Was I abused then, when a child? Were the punishment beatings abuse? There, that's come out of the blue, eh? But God help me, I can't remember; and if they were they made a man of me. They hand you down these skills and traits, the family, that's what we all dread, isn't it? You've your father's eyes, your mother's smile, just like your old man I can hear him saying it, a chip off the old block yes and o you little chubbycheeks such a charmer you'll be breaking women's hearts when the day comes, you've your father's alcoholism and your mother's lung disease your father's nervous condition and your mother's bladder weakness, yes it's a real family concern, plenty to look forward to. When you bury them you say none of this. Penelope, Odysseus, Telemachus, what a family that was! Insane, to a man. You couldn't make it up. No, mine was ordinary, I realised that after the years, nothing special or notorious about it. There was a book I liked once, liked enough to read a few pages anyway; it starts with a child, the mother dies, the father's no good, there's a stepmother and then, when the father dies, a stepfather, and they are cold, they give him no love. Mine was nothing like that, we had larks what larks in between the privations nothing to complain of far better off than most think of those people starving in where was it? Leatherhead? no Africa that was it The Third World all those children with huge bellies and limbs like sticks no we had nothing like that we were clothed and fed and told to wash behind our ears and beaten and so on. Bliss, was it? in that dawn to be alive. No, you had to wait a bit to get that; childhood's more ordinary. Hardly worth bothering about really. No, really.

I feel I should put this in some sort of order (but which sort? the right sort? the wrong sort? alphabetical order? chronological? order of merit?) but why? Not for posterity- there isn't one; and surely not for my contemporaries or coevals if any of them are still alive, for why would they want to traipse through all this, whether ordered or disordered? And as for trying to put it in order for my own benefit! Where would I start? And for what?- so that I can approach death in good conscience, with the unction of having put my affairs in order on my nob? Anointing my nob. I ask where did I start, but I did start (see p.1) and it's as good a start as any, a memory either true or false probably false most memories are, and one that mattered, had significance; unless it didn't matter, was insignificant. Bugger, I'm getting disgruntled now; when I was no worse than gruntled before. I should put these ramblings in some sort of order. But what order; the order of the bath, order of the day? Bath, eat, dress, yes it's obvious where to start. But carry on?

It's simple enough this writing in the first person confused and confusing though it be, but I thank GodinwhomIhavenofaith, I get/would get down on my knees to thank GodIWIHNF, I have not confused myself or complicated matters more by introducing any other false narrators. Imagine- I employ the words bath, eat, dress, and congratulate myself how clear and simple and unambiguous I am being, but look at it this way
 I bath/eat/dress
 He/she/it bathes/eats/dresses
Why o why o why is it I Bath, but He Bathes? answer me that. You can't so don't bother trying. And if we got on to Theyno, don't. They eats, they eat. God help us I despair. We didn't have this in my day yes we did. But why is it I Eat She Eats? It's like we want to create division and argument and internecine conflict (internecine war- war between nieces stop tittering at the back and you might learn something). I'll go back- I gets up in't mornin' 'n' I baths 'n' puts on me clothes 'n' I eats. I breaks my fast. There that's simple enough isn't it? Even a tin-eared cloth-headed obstinate backwardlooking stick-in-the-mud stubborn-as-a-mule clot such as I can understand it. A fool such as I.

I can't say I enjoyed that digression especially or even at all, but I think it was useful to write it down and clear the air somewhat even if only by making it murkier (murking it?

murkifying it?). There were once rumours, I was told years later, that I had married a can-can dancer from Preston, or if not that, a Presbyterian fish-gutter in Ross and Cromarty, but these were wild and unsubstantiated, for what would I have been doing in Preston? how would I have come to meet a Presbyterian? and how could such a thing have happened without my having any knowledge of it? No, this just shows how people cannot help but deceive themselves as well as others, but it's slandering and therefore damaging. For all I know they went on from that to tell each other I had been press-ganged or was scraping a living as an Elvis Presley impersonator. You see what I mean? You see how this works. Fortunately this all passed me by- it was the year I was supply teaching in Ditchling- and I was able to laugh about it when I was told. But now I can't. I wish the rumours had been true. Not the fish-gutter. The other one.

All the talk is of dying with dignity, by which is meant not dying in a pool of your own shit (well of course your own shit, idiot!), unable to reach the call-bell for the nurse; meaning, and don't take it from me, there are books and books and learned papers in journals, peer-reviewed and referenced and the rest of it, that those in attendance on the dying refrain from slapping them or swearing at them every time they soil the bed or puke on the clean nightshirt, also from keeping visitors away from their Loved Ones six days of the week. All this talk, not to mention acting on it, drawing up Care Plans and so on, not to mention either the whole fucking fantasy of anyone's having Loved Ones, does not inspire me. No. No- I think...dignity of this kind...does not appeal to me...does not accord with my wishes. I want to stay here in my own bed with an ashtray and a bottle of something and Mozart or one of those fellows playing softly, and that is where and how I want to die, and don't whatever you do or don't do let any of the so-called Loved Ones come fidgeting and fannying around, wiping my tongue with a sponge and squeezing my hand and pretending not to be disgusted at the sight of me or the smell. Yes that's the way, unless I am caught short and end up on the floor having failed to make it to the jakes; or I make it as far as the forest and get eaten by wild animals of some kind- lions, jackals, wolves, rats. Flies. And if I am found like that and they say He died without dignity, what a final judgement that will be. He died without dignity, the swine. He died without dignity ergo he must have lived without dignity. What kind of a fellow have we been harbouring at our supper tables all these years? I'll be dead and won't care, but I feel for my relicts, if such there be. I can't help but think it will redound on them, this judgement. They will have to live with it, the unknown rumourmongers, the can-can dancers, the fishwives. Harry. Jesus, what am I thinking? I want her to be there but she won't and there is absolutely no reason why she would or could or should be there, so what am I thinking? She was there at the beginning. She knows the meaning of life.

I have too many questions that have no answers. Why did Harry read my diary? Why did she tell me she had read it? Why did I write it? Why was I letting myself get the hots for Lily when I was having such a great time with Harry? Was I actually having such a great time with Harry? I could still, now, even at this late stage, try to answer some of these, perhaps with the help of a psychiatrist or a priest (no, not a priest) but what would be the point? There, that's another question I can't answer. When I was at school, at the age of perhaps twelve or thirteen, the teacher who took us for R.I. or R.E., whichever it was, introduced, for a short time, a box into which you could pop questions anonymously. I can't remember any of them, and I can't remember what if any instructions he gave us about what kind of questions to ask, so I don't know if he was expecting questions about sex (Dear Sir I keep getting a tingling in my loins when I see Miss de Sousa taking the girls for netball. Is this normal?), or religious doubt (Dear Sir Do you really believe in all this bollocks?), or the more personal (Dear Sir Why don't you ever brush the dandruff off your shoulders? It looks disgusting); but it might be useful to have such a box now into which I might pop my questions. Dear Sir Why did Harry fall out with me just because I wanted to have sexual intercourse with her best friend? I can't remember his name now, but he should be able to answer that, shouldn't he? Of course he's no longer about, in fact he's probably dead, so it will just have to stay in the box and not trouble me any more. Then what will I do?

But don't misunderstand, this is not important, or to be more precise, these complications are, were not, important. It's what's simple I'm trying to get at- the day we first met, the few hours we spent alone together, what happened, what it felt like. But I can't write about it; it will be inaccurate in every detail, not to mention a pack of lies. How can you write about the seminal hours of your life and expect to get it right? You can't. Look at it this way- the simple things! What did she look like? I don't know. What was her voice like? I don't know. There was something on her left breast- a wrinkle? a scar was it? She had dark hair. That's the best I can do. Really.

Enough! Enough questions for God's sake. I wish I had the balls to write I hereby solemnly swear that there will be no more questions in this manuscript come hell or high water but there's no point it can't be done. (Already I want to ask what does hereby mean?) It's like hoping the telephone will never ring again or if it does that it will be a simple matter such as news that someone has died, not one of those awful calls when somebody wants to make an arrangement with you, ask if you can be at such and such a place at such a time on such a day; or somebody who asks your advice (without actually wanting it); or somebody who wants to tell you my wife has left me or I'm having a midlife crisis or I've got cancer; and whoever it is expects you to say something! What a demand that is; you can't call it friendship, telephoning you at any hour of the day, asking questions, telling you things, expecting you to say something. No, better if they just left a message, such friends- I'm dead; nice to have known you. No flowers please. There, I've done it again, got on to death, when I thought I was talking about questions and trying to do away with them. What's the point of questions? There are no answers. Only more questions.

It was lunchtime a short while ago. What a lovely word it is- lunchtime. The last moment of hope in the day. I popped over to the Co-op and bought a mini egg sandwich and thought about the days that are no more while I munched. It is a good thing to have these little bites to eat. You don't look like a savage as you do when you take a bite and find bits of egg and crumbs on your chin and your fingers and down your front and so on. In your crutch. You just pop it into your mouth and munch. Very dainty. But yes, even a small pleasure like this gets the old memory-box spewing up its filth- childhood and so on. O to be eighteen again and have a second chance; that's what's behind it; but, by Jupiter, the thought of being eighteen again and having to relive all of those days and years between then and now, it's beyond fathom or below it or whatever. Unfathomable anyhow.

Funny thing being born a boy. They put you in shirt and trousers, not skirts and dresses; pants not knickers; cut your hair instead of putting it in pipe cleaners to curl it. Had they done the other thing and put me into a skirt, let my hair grow down to my waist, I don't know, I suppose I'd have turned out different. I wouldn't have appreciated it. And yet I still- no, not still, I've only just thought of it- think what if? What if I hadn't been set in my ways Right From The Start? What then? I coulda been a contender. Mighta.

You might wonder or I might wonder why I am writing in this old-fashioned style. I just want to put these things down before the world comes to its end. Is it plausible however, you might ask. Is it plausible? Poets cannot be plausible; they are mythographers, and myths, surely, are no longer any use in trying to increase our understanding, to understand how to increase our understanding. So the question of plausibility is, perhaps, also of no use. Ask yourself- is some or all of what you have read up to this point plausible? Is some or all of it implausible? Put like that, it doesn't matter at all. Any attempt to state What Happened, in the past, will fail, for now, at least. So forgive me if I begin the next chunk of this failed attempt to describe, failed attempt to remember, failed attempt to be impartial, in this way-

It was the sheep-shearing season, a busy time for all, when Mum and Dad had little time for us children and we were left to our own devices and desires, our own experiments, none of which were designed better or improved upon those of our forebears. These days everyone talks of wanting closure. No not everyone but still wouldn't it be better to want the opposite- opening(s)? O God I'm wandering, not as bad as Dostoevsky but- far far wide. Far and wide, yes, I admit to both, but what is the alternative? Peeking through a keyhole? Seeing only a few things that might give you a clue about what goes on in there? No, let us go far and wide, explore the nether regions no not nether outer. Outer regions. What is the point of sticking here any longer in the room with the window and the cooker and the kettle and the refrigerator and the tea bags and the sofa and the comfy chair and the uncomfy one and the table I sometimes bother to sit and eat at and the bookshelves and the bloody books and the paper and the pen and the ink and I? And I, the centre of this plausiverse, for how could the kettle do anything useful or at all were I, the primum mobile, not here to ignite it? Shear those sheep, keep those old traditions, keep them alive. The traditions and the sheep too.

Buy why failure? Why do I call it that? I have lived all the days of my life, got out of bed every morning, washed, eaten my breakfast, dressed myself, gone to work and so on; even exercised, modified my diet, cut down on the booze and so on; married, had children, had the children baptised and schooled and so on; even sat at the wife's deathbed, chief mourner at her funeral and so on. Parents too, though not children God I hope to be spared that, that would finish me I should think. No more questions then, no more self-examinations and wrist-slitting about failure, my failure, as if anybody noticed or cared. There's no escaping thinking about yourself though, you can't do otherwise no matter how much you pray or flagellate yourself or both. And your children never let you forget you. Merciless they are. Children.

I'm terrified. I may not sound it but I am. What a thing it is to be merciless and to have no mercy taken on you. Nothing could be worse. No- many more things could be worse, but just at the moment it seems to me that nothing could be worse than my having no mercy and no-one- neither gods nor men- having mercy upon me. Salve Regina etc etc. Forgive me. Bollocks. It's an odd thing really- fear. How many times in my life have I been afraid? and how few have I had anything to be afraid of? Of which to be afraid. Nothing ever happens. The occasional mugging, heart attack, divorce etc but nothing worse and not often; no, seldom does life live down to your expectations. Once you've got used to the idea, that it's not so marvellous, this short flight through the world. Arrival, departure. Nothing to be frightened of. What a thought though! Nothing of which to be frightened! What- what no but what what if she doesn't remember me, at all, not even when I prompt her and say you must- that day we met, when you invited me into your room and played that song you loved- you've got to hear this, you said, and then trembling I put my hand on you and you welcomed it. Don't be afraid it was as though you had said, and I've never been afraid since. And then you threw the bloody crockery at me. No, not then; later. I was afraid then.

And what if she refuses to recognise my claim? My entire life will be shown to be meaningless. What can I tell my friends? How can I sit at table with them, gorging and laugh- ing, all that civilised middle-class behaviour? These feelings about what happened surely depend upon knowing, remem- bering accurately, what happened? If I can't, the feelings can't be the right ones, can they? The right ones for me, for My Self. Feelings, surely, don't have a life of their own? Perhaps I have fallen for the narrative fallacy, that fiction (autobiog- raphy, it is sometimes called) unreels like a chain in which you can see every link. When the fiction ends and you can see the last link, you can also see that it is connected, even if at some distance, to the first. What does this prove? Don't be daft- I'm not trying to prove anything, just trying to take one step not even a step a shuffle in the direction of understand- ing One Bloody Thing In My Life! There. Put that in your pipe. Smoke it.

Were I to jump to a conclusion which of course I will not, having been advised against so doing all my life, that is, supposing I remember anything at all about my life; after all, you often hear said- that's You, not I - Don't go jumping to conclusions, but you never hear said My advice is to jump to conclusions, so it's a kind of tautology (saying Don't jump etc) or its opposite, antonym or whatever. So were I to jump, were I able to jump rather than just shuffle in these loose-fitting slippers I wear that I probably shouldn't even shuffle in never mind jump, were I to...what then? I've lost my thread now dammit same as always. Go back- surely this, surely that...the chain...understanding...jump...the slippers...Well, jumping is, paradoxically, a sign of laziness, not vigour- I can't be bothered to put in the brainwork required for understanding, so I'll jump, perhaps even jump blindfold. Hope. For the best.

Silly to talk of conclusions when there are no such things. I cannot go through this again I tell myself and then I go through it again. Am I helpless then, or do I want to? What if I don't want to- would I have it land on me again against my will? This reminder that there was someone once a long time ago, someone like me but different, the same but dead (yes, dead; don't be shocked, that man is gone, unmourned- of course unmourned!- for why would anyone mourn someone who has not died?) You see that I still ask questions, in spite of myself; it's because I have no answers, no certainties. I cannot go through this again; I go through it again. There's no point, it's not as if I learn anything, solve anything, whatever that might mean. It's an affirmation and whatever the antonym of affirmation is- nullification, perhaps? No I can't mean that- I am perhaps unacquainted with grief; I am less than the sum of my parts. It isn't that I want to see her again, to hear or imagine what her life has been like, to know what she looks like now, to know what she sounds like and of what she can speak. What could she say that might please me or satisfy the depraved hunger I have? Nor do I wish to relive the past; neither relive it just as it happened, nor with the so-called benefit of hindsight. No. To see what I have always somehow seen and joy in it. Revelation.

There were ponies in the field out back. I have no vivid memory of what they looked like, but stunted, I think, un-attractive. It would be no wonder then were I to have felt lower in caste than my contemporaries, even were that manifestly not so. But their parents had cars and gave them, my friends and acquaintances, cash money when they visited. There, that's all the misery there's going to be in this memoir. It's always going to strike a false note, this burrowing for memories I don't remember and don't want to be reminded of. God forbid that I should stumble across the truth. And then have to work out how to forgive myself. How many priests and therapists would I have to pay to learn that dark art? At what price?

Ideally my idea would be to press on with this writing until the last possible moment, but we don't live in an ideal world and never will, so we must live with the one we have for as long as is necessary. For as long as I am able, however, I mean to go on pestering the old questions, like a dog with a filthy, hairless, torn-open tennis ball. Was it that my mother was too busy to come up and kiss me goodnight one night? When I was small, impressionable. That would be a good question to ask if not to answer. Well, the questions have no ideal answers, do they now? There was something though, surely, that stamped its dye on my flank, in a place that few people would ever inspect, but a daily reminder to me that love is impossible. Irreparable. Indispensable. All the fault of my mother's delinquency? Unlikely. Just the way of things.

We've all had to learn not to sleep during this latest or possibly final crisis. Eighteen months and counting, though counting is easy enough if you do it only once a month; it's when every second counts that your nerve is inclined to snap, your judgement become leg-weary; and counting the seconds you are not sleeping puts you at the end of your rope there's no doubt about that. A Lear-like madness might be the crock of gold at the foot of that particular rainbow. I hate not sleeping: the very blackest of dreams can visit you, have you tossing and rolling like a round thing on a ship's deck in a storm, wake you with a spittle-flecked start and have you rummaging in the penance-box of your conscience for the source of the sin you suspect you cried out in your sleep. Not that you slept.

The maddening thing well not maddening but cross-making, is the not being able to dream the dreams you want to dream. Neither waking nor sleeping do the images and situations and climaxes and denouements come as I should like. And then not to remember the face of the loved one, this the most terrible aspect of grief, this realising, this making-real of the thing that you cannot, will not, refuse to believe in, but which your mind, that lifelong betrayer, that Judas, refuses to let you not. And once the betrayal has taken place, once witnessed and memorialised, there is no going back, no escape, not even into dreams, not even into dreams you write yourself when you're awake. I can't remember her face. I can't remember her face, that giant step down into the Hades of forgetting. Not, however, a straight journey down, for grieving is never over until you die; it has to be done so many times, so that everything is properly grieved for. And the same is true too for remembering and forgetting. You can't just forget the once; you have to forget day after day. Dreadful business.

Paradoxically, or antithetically- the latter I think or at least prefer- perhaps this is why I can't forget Harry; because I do remember her face. It can't be her real face, of course; it's not as if I have a photograph to compare; but I remember her face; simple as that. Her face was a simple one, the type you can't forget. Keep writing. You're not nearly there yet. She has stayed the same age. Neither have I.

Yes keep writing there's no bloody point but it's best to keep on there's no other way to bring her back not even this one until of course we meet in the afterlife when all shall be well and all shall be well and even more perfect and wonderful than it was then, when she was a young woman called Harry and I was whoever I was, for a while, and even that while, however long it lasted, never as perfect and wonderful as it was the day I met her- have I told that? Can't remember, and can't be bothered to look back. I'll tell about it now. It was like this-

- Like this. Like what? It's memory so cannot be relied upon but it was like this. There was a woman whose name I can't recall from Bristol blonde I used to be in her room how did that happen? I don't know. She would go for a bath and be back in five minutes or even less; it was a boast of hers that she could bathe so quickly. I didn't fancy her. She was going away probably back home to Bristol and let me have her room for the weekend and before she went she introduced me to Harry who was just up the corridor and said Harry will look after you. Oooooh. Yes, that's the first bit, I'm sure of it. Sure? Don't be daft.

These days I want to sleep and dream and never wake up. It wasn't always like this. It is said, I suppose, that there is no point in being afraid of death as it's just like sleep, but it isn't, or as far as I can tell it isn't. I can't tell, of course I can't, never having been dead, but it can't be the same. Yes, sometimes I feel that I'd like to sleep and dream and never wake up, or wake up intermittently to remind myself what a good time I'm having and then drop off again. You can't live like that though. Not for long. Not at all.

Funny- I always wanted to be called Jess and so I was, though fools of friends and family insisted my real names are ********** Jeremy. I won't tell you what the first, or Christian, name is, or was; I never use it, and I hate it. Okay it's a saint's name, but that won't help you. I'll give you a clue it's not St. P****. Yes, Jess and Harry, Harry and Jess, they sound all right, don't they? You can imagine, can you not, saying Hi Jess, Harry- how are the kids? How long have you two been together now thirty years is it forty? You're the perfect couple you were made for each other. Bye Harry, bye Jess. You can. I can't.

That was the first bit, the blonde from Bristol who took only five minutes to bathe leaving for Bristol and me in the hands of Harry, whom I had not met before. That's the easy bit and I'm avoiding getting on to what happened next because it's the important bit and I want to do it justice. I wanted to do it justice then but I was callow youth but now I'm callow age and like Master Shallow, slippered and dribbling and recalling the chimes at midnight when he was too drunk and timid to do anything but pay his small coin to the bona-robas- this is how it ends up. Good to remember the bells though, that would be a comfort, enough to say this life was worth living. But justice? The idea! I was a party to these doings, so how can I be the judge of them, weighing what scraps of evidence might still be gathered? No, not even evidence, you know that; only the pestilent persistence of my pigheaded memory. Do what justice? Pah!

Arrival. The bus station. Ah! Now we're there! What a gorgeous, filthy smell that was to welcome me. It smelled of youth, desire, growing up, whetting my appetite for all the gorgeous, filthy experiences I was on the verge of experiencing. It smelled of men not boys. I would sit upstairs on the bus, marking off what soon became landmarks. You came up out of town and then it levelled off, and you looked out at fields and farms, and you stopped here and there- places with a pub and a post office- church- and people would get off and on and the bus conductor would step off to smoke a cigarette and say good morning to someone he knew, and there would be laughter. When we were near we began our descent. Ugh! I am trying to be realistic and it stinks. What does realism have to do with this? Realism has nothing to do with any of this. (Harry!) How can you lie about so much and at the same time - idem tempus?- suggest, pretend, assert even, that you have been telling the truth? It won't wash. But I had crossed a line, that was certain, there was no going back even had I dinged the bell, got off the bus, walked- walked!- all the way back to the bus station, what then? I could never have washed that smell of diesel out of my memory. It's too long ago. It changed everything. The smell of Harry. Others too. You can't walk back the past. Ain't that the truth?

TWO VERSIONS

In Homer's Iliad, which is about the war between the Trojans and their allies and the Greeks and their allies that took place in about 750bc, there are about 275 deaths. This might sound a lot but there are far more in the Old Testament- 270,000 in the Book of Judges alone, and that is only 21 chapters long. However: the first death in the Iliad comes when Antilochus, a Greek, kills Echepolus, a Trojan.

His name is not Antilochus
He never thrust his sword into a Trojan throat
With such force that it cut through the roof of his tongue
And went up through teeth, bone, eyes until it pierced
his brain
And blood flowed from the Trojan's head, and darkness
closed his eyes

No, his name is unknown, but I shall call him Danny
He deserves a name
We see him first from behind, walking in the middle of
the road.
It's all right, it's not a busy road, it's the road in which I live

And back up which I walk this Sunday morning with the
paper and a pint of milk

I watch him- not quite staggering, but swaying as he walks
And I watch him stop, lean to one side, and place
An empty beer-bottle upright on the ground, and walk on.
I call to him Hey, don't leave your rubbish in the street.
Without turning to look, he raises an arm, his middle
finger thrust up from his fist.
Maddened, I shout again- but, before I tell you this
I must explain that I am not, though I feel like his natural
enemy,
A fighting man; and, even if I had gods to protect me,
I could ask them only to spirit me away-
I shout again: That doesn't seem much like an apology.

And then, because he is- no, not staggering, but swaying,
Whereas I am upright, purposeful, I overtake him, and
As I pass, he turns his head, and I see a burned, un-
shaven face,
Drink-blurred eyes, drink-twisted lips
Through which he snarls the words "Muslim Fucking
Cunt".

I hurry on, and past my door- I don't want him to see
where I live.
I walk on to the high road, to the bus stop where
I pretend to read the timetable, my heart thumping.
He- the man who is not Antilokhos and whom I have
decided to call Danny-

Approaches, his hands empty, the words HATE and
LOVE tattooed on his knuckles

And while I pretend to be interested in the timetable
And while I pretend not to have noticed him there,
He speaks, and in a low respectful growl, says this:
"I'm sorry", which surprises me so much I abandon all
pretence
And I turn my head and look him in the eyes.

He looks away, down at the ground, down at, I suppose,
his shame.
"I don't know what I'm saying at the moment
"I don't know where I am or what I'm doing
"I've just come back"
And I can't remember if he said so, or if it was just obvious

That he had just come back from fighting the war in Iraq
And whatever he has seen or whatever he has done
Or whatever has been done to him
Is in his nightmares, and not only in the night
But in the day-time too

As if a prophecy, invited in jest, had come all too true.
How changed he is, unless he is not changed at all-
Perhaps he is the same as he has always been.
I imagine a worse-than-mischievous schoolboy, a not-
quite-criminal teenager
A good-for-nothing-but-cannon-fodder young man

And now this shell-shocked victim of the war; and who was I to know
What guilt what fear what horrors have made him this?
"I'm sorry" he says again, "that I spoke to you like that.
"I don't even know what I said. They're just words
"They don't mean anything." We shake hands

And I must have wished him well. I remember
Him as often as I remember old friends
And I wonder what became of him. I wonder what became of him that day
After I left him and went home and washed my hands
And breakfasted and wondered what I should have done to help.

The Kipling Version

O gallant are our soldiers; they are heroes every one
From brigadier to private underneath the eastern sun
And when they bring the bodies back we dip our heads and pray
We'll even shake our pockets out to help them on their way

And if the limbless veterans can turn their lives around
We'll read their heartbreak stories in the newspapers,

spellbound
Of how they beat the drink and drugs and coped with
the divorce
And when they're asked for reasons- well; it's for the kids,
of course

But when the bugle's lowered and the colours have been
struck
And the men are back in civvies and adjusting to their luck
There's some whose nightmares stalk them through the
cities' crowded streets
And they are not dreams of brav'ry or humanitarian feats

I'm thinking of a chap I saw one Sunday years ago
He was rolling down the street half-cut; at breakfast-time
y'know
Not my concern, of course, if fellers choose to get pie-eyed
But dropping rubbish on the street's a thing I can't abide

So when I watched him bend and place his bottle on the
ground
I saw red and I shouted out Oi! You there, turn around
An' pick your rubbish up and leave the street a tidy place.
He didn't turn around; he didn't even change his pace

But he answered me by sticking up two fingers in the air
That really got my dander up and made my temper flare
That's no kind of apology I shouted loud and clear
I was so much in the right I thought the street would
give a cheer

But no; it was just me and him; and though I'd been so bold
As I drew 'longside of him I felt my blood run cold
For he turned to me a face so black, half-dead, half-'live
he seemed
And from his cracked and blistered lips some foul abuse
he screamed

You Muslim this, you Muslim that; it made no sense to me
For I'm a white-skinned atheist, and as liberal as can be
But, sense or not, it frightened me and I hurried past
my door
I didn't want him coming round and cursing me the more

So I went up to the high road, thought there'd be more
people there
For I don't mind admitting it, he'd given me a scare
Thought I'll wait here at the bus stop until he's gone away
But I'd only been there seconds when I saw him come
my way

I saw his eyes- Lord, what a sight! for I saw horrors there
I saw his burned, unshaven face; I saw his matted hair
I smelled his clothes- from sleeping rough, he stank to
heaven above
I saw his tattoed knuckles with the message HATE and
LOVE

He came up close and muttered, while his eyes looked at
the ground

"I'm sorry" were the words he spoke, 'n I choked up at
the sound
"I don't know what I'm saying, and I don't know what
I mean
"I don't know what I'm doing, and I don't know where
I've been

"I've only just come back, you see, and everything seems
wrong
"I can't go home and let them see this man they thought
so strong
"Start crying like a baby when the lights go out at night
"I'm only good for fighting; now I don't know who to
fight."

Well, God knows what he'd seen or done or what's been
done to him
But I shook his hand and wished him well and felt my
eyelids brim
"I'm sorry" he said one last time and turned and walked
away
And I went home with my newspaper and that's all I
can say

*Estimates of the number of casualties during the invasion in
Iraq vary widely*

ABOUT THE AUTHOR

Anthony White is a spoken-word poet. Born in London in 1954, for most of his life he was a nurse. Now retired, he lives in Folkestone, where we performs his work, mostly with Poets' Corner Folkestone, of which he is a founding member. He has also written and performed solo shows at Faversham Fringe Festival. He has published two collections, Miserable Love Poetry and Other Poems (2022) and The Deathbed Poet and Other Poems (2023).